S.S.F. Public Library
West Orange
840 West Orange Ave.
South San Francisco, CA 94080

Sou... ...co... Library
0048 10046699 8

JUL 1 5

D0427240

FRECKLEFACE STRAWBERRY
Lunch, or WHAT'S THAT?

For kids who love hot dogs
—J.M.

Text copyright © 2015 by Julianne Moore
Jacket art and interior illustrations copyright © 2015 by LeUyen Pham

All rights reserved. Published in the United States by Doubleday, an imprint of
Random House Children's Books, a division of Penguin Random House LLC, New York.

Doubleday and the colophon are registered trademarks of Penguin Random House LLC.

Visit us on the Web! randomhousekids.com

Educators and librarians, for a variety of teaching tools, visit us at RHTeachersLibrarians.com

Library of Congress Cataloging-in-Publication Data
Moore, Julianne.
Freckleface Strawberry : lunch, or what's that? / Julianne Moore ; illustrated by LeUyen Pham.
pages cm. — (Step into reading. Step 2)
Summary: "Freckleface Strawberry and Windy Pants Patrick are wary of the school lunch."
—Provided by publisher.
ISBN 978-0-385-39192-4 (trade) — ISBN 978-0-375-97366-6 (lib. bdg.) —
ISBN 978-0-385-39191-7 (pbk.) — ISBN 978-0-385-39193-1 (ebook)
[1. Best friends—Fiction. 2. Friendship—Fiction. 3. Luncheons—Fiction. 4. School lunchrooms,
cafeterias, etc.—Fiction.] I. Pham, LeUyen, illustrator. II. Title. III. Title: Lunch, or what's that?
PZ7.M78635Frp 2015
[E]—dc23
2014040653

MANUFACTURED IN MALAYSIA

10 9 8 7 6 5 4 3 2 1

Random House Children's Books supports the First Amendment and celebrates the right to read.

FRECKLEFACE STRAWBERRY
Lunch, or WHAT'S THAT?

by Julianne Moore

illustrated by LeUyen Pham

Doubleday Books for Young Readers

Chapter 1

Freckleface Strawberry
and Windy Pants Patrick
both loved to eat lunch.

They loved
to eat
hot dogs.

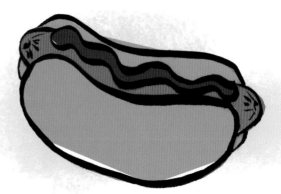

They loved
to eat
grilled cheese.

They loved to eat
peanut butter and jelly.

They loved to eat
chicken fingers.

They loved
to eat noodles.

They loved to eat.

They loved to eat lunch,
but they did NOT
love to eat lunch
in the lunch room.

9

Chapter 2

One day,
Freckleface Strawberry
and Windy Pants Patrick
went to the lunch room.

Freckleface Strawberry
got into the lunch line.
She put her lunch
on the tray.

She sat down next to
Windy Pants.

Freckleface Strawberry
was ready to eat.

"What is that?"
Windy Pants Patrick asked.
"That?" said Freckleface.
"That is lunch."

"I know that is lunch,"
said Windy Pants.
"But WHAT is it?"
"I do not know,"
said Freckleface.

Chapter 3

Then Winnie sat down.
"What is that?" said Winnie.
"What?" said Freckleface.
"That," said Winnie.

"That is lunch,"
  said Freckleface.
"Oh," said Winnie.
"But what is it?"
  Freckleface said sadly,
"I do not know."

Then Noah sat down.

"How is lunch?" Noah yelled.

"I do not know,"

said Freckleface.

"Why not?"
asked Noah loudly.
"Because THAT is lunch,"
said Freckleface.
She pointed at her tray.

"That?" cried Noah.
"THAT is lunch?"
"YES!" shouted Freckleface,
Windy Pants, and Winnie.

"Shhhhhhhhhhhhh!"
said the lunch room teacher.
"No yelling in
the lunch room.
Only lunch eating."

"Well, it IS time for
    lunch eating," Freckleface
    Strawberry whispered.
"It is MY lunch.
    I GUESS I will eat it."

Chapter 4

Windy Pants Patrick,
Winnie, and Noah
were very, very quiet.
Freckleface Strawberry
ate her lunch.

Windy Pants, Winnie,
and Noah watched her eat.
Windy Pants, Winnie,
and Noah were
very, very curious.

Freckleface Strawberry
chewed a long time.
Finally, Windy Pants
Patrick said, "What is it?"

Freckleface Strawberry
shook her head.
"I do not know,"
she said. . . .

"But I LIKE it!"

And then they all
ate lunch.